Once Upon a Garden

Lucy's Light

Jo Rooks

MAGINATION PRESS 🍂 WASHINGTON, DC
American Psychological Association

For Lucy-Jo.—*JR*

Copyright © 2019 by Jo Rooks. Published in 2019
by Magination Press, an imprint of the American
Psychological Association. All rights reserved. Except
as permitted under the United States Copyright Act of
1976, no part of this publication may be reproduced or
distributed in any form or by any means, or stored in a
database or retrieval system, without the prior written
permission of the publisher.

Magination Press is a registered trademark of the
American Psychological Association. Order books at
maginationpress.org or call 1-800-374-2721.

Book design by Gwen Grafft

Printed by Lake Book Manufacturing, Inc., Melrose Park, IL

Library of Congress Cataloging-in-Publication Data
Names: Rooks, Jo, author, illustrator.
Title: Lucy's light / by Jo Rooks.
Description: Washington, DC : Magination Press, [2019] |
    Series: [Once upon a garden] | "American Psychological
    Association." | Summary: Lucy the lightning bug hides
    the fact that she cannot light up but when her team is
    in danger, her excellent flying skills are all she needs.
Identifiers: LCCN 2018047253| ISBN 9781433830884
    (hardcover) | ISBN 1433830884 (hardcover)
Subjects: | CYAC: Ability—Fiction. | Fireflies—Fiction. |
    Secrets—Fiction.
Classification: LCC PZ7.1.R66854 Luc 2019 | DDC [E]—
dc23 LC record available at https://lccn.loc.gov/2018047253

Manufactured in the United States of America
10 9 8 7 6 5 4 3 2 1

Lucy was a lightning bug.

… and the most talented
flyer in the squad.

She could perform perfect loop-da-loops …

and zig-zag through the trees at terrific speed!

ZOOOM!

Everyone was very impressed.

One day, Miss Sparks had some news.

"It's time to learn … **NIGHT** flying!" she said.
"Practice is at sunset."

Everyone was **very** excited.

Everyone except Lucy.

Because, Lucy was a lightning bug
who **didn't** light up ... not even a flicker!

Whoever heard of a lightning bug
who doesn't light up?" said Lucy.

"Just follow us!" said Fliss kindly.

"Maybe my light will appear if I fly in a **different** way," thought Lucy.

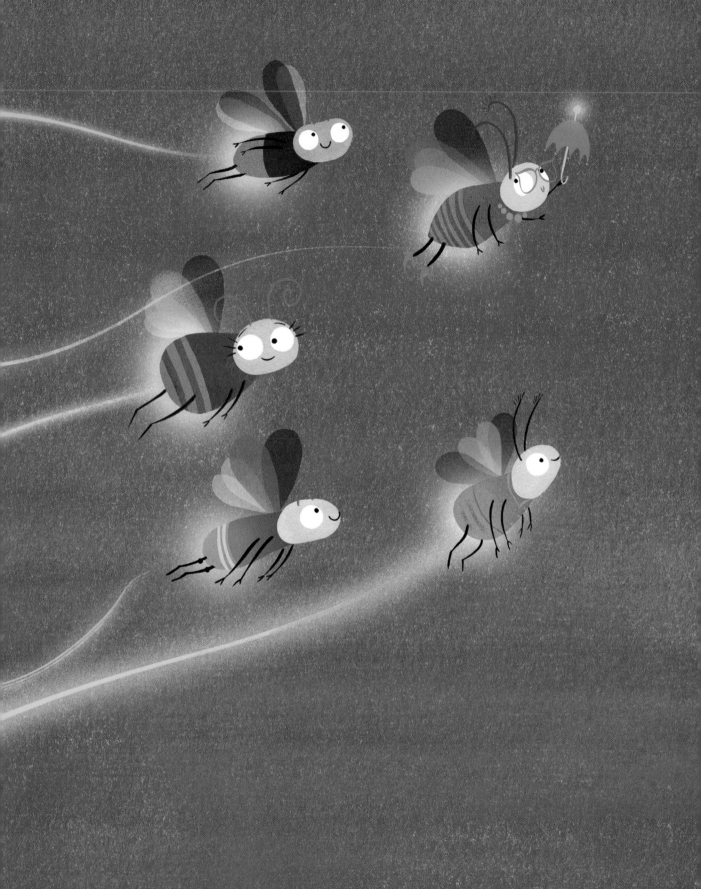

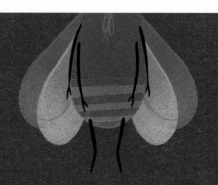

So Lucy flew **higher**

lower

faster

slower

Round and round …

… and upside-down

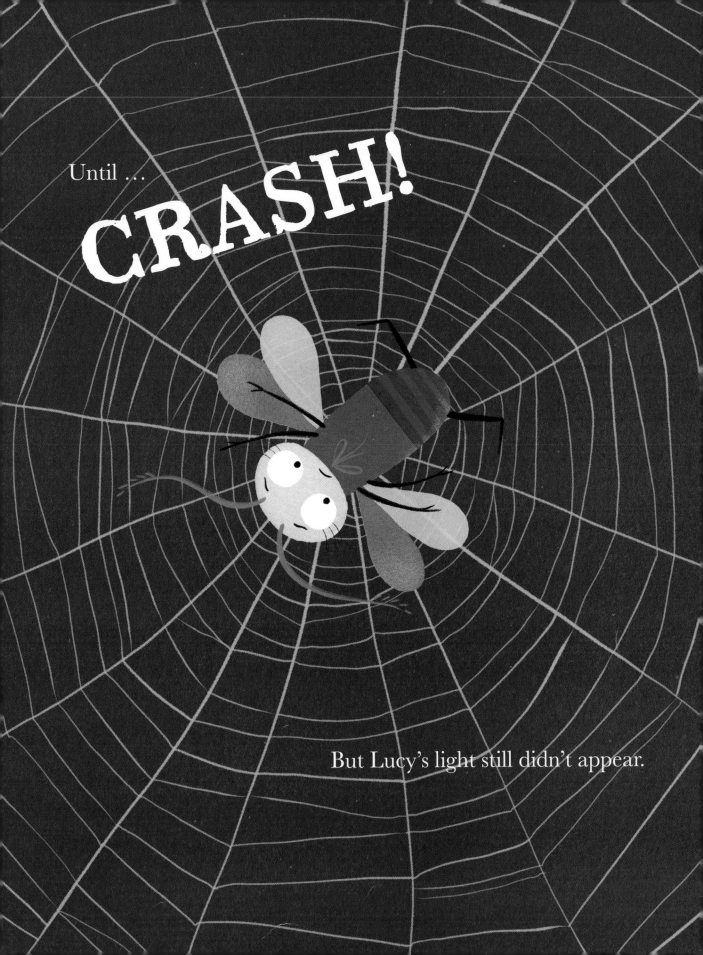

Until ... CRASH!

But Lucy's light still didn't appear.

When Lucy had caught up with the others,
they were having a rest on a **big** rock.

"It turns out I'm not a lightning bug after all,"
said Lucy, "I'm just an **ordinary** bug."

She was about to fly home
when the rock ... **croaked**!

"They'll brighten up our gloomy bog,"
said the newt.

"What about **that** one?"
said the frog pointing to Lucy.

"No, that's just an **ordinary** bug," laughed the toad.

All of a sudden, Lucy felt an inner strength
burning inside her.

She knew there was only one thing to do.

ZOOOM!

She frightened the frog.

WHIZZ!

She dizzied the newt.

NEOOM!

She terrified the toad!

"Now, hop it!" said Lucy.

They were so scared that they ran off back to their bog.

Lucy used her super strength to set the
lightning bugs free and everyone cheered!

They were so thankful to Lucy,
that she was given a special medal.

"You're no ordinary bug, Lucy."
said Miss Sparks "You're the bravest
bug in the **whole** garden."

And she never forgot that doing
a good deed will always make
you shine bright!